Daddy's
LITTLE HELPER

Darrin Morris

ISBN 978-1-09806-050-3 (paperback)
ISBN 978-1-09809-986-2 (hardcover)
ISBN 978-1-09806-051-0 (digital)

Christian Faith Publishing, Inc.
832 Park Avenue
Meadville, PA 16335
www.christianfaithpublishing.com

Printed in the United States of America

I would like to dedicate this book to my boys, Dillon Gene Morris and Darrin Lance Morris. Their great spirit toward life and love for me inspired me to write this book to show them every little moment we share means the world to me. I love them with all my heart and will always cherish time spent with them past, present, and future.

A special thanks to my wife Lavada Morris and great friend Jim Ryder for their wisdom and encouragement.

I would also like to thank my friends and family for their support and encouragement.

My Lord and Savior, Jesus Christ, without whom nothing is possible, but with him all things are.

Daddy's little helper
as morning breaks.

We start the day off
by eating pancakes.

5

Daddy's little helper
his right hand man.

I help daddy out
best I can.

Daddy's little helper
when things aren't safe.

I help remove boards,
just in case.

Daddy's little helper
even on the go.

I help Daddy shop
at the hardware store.

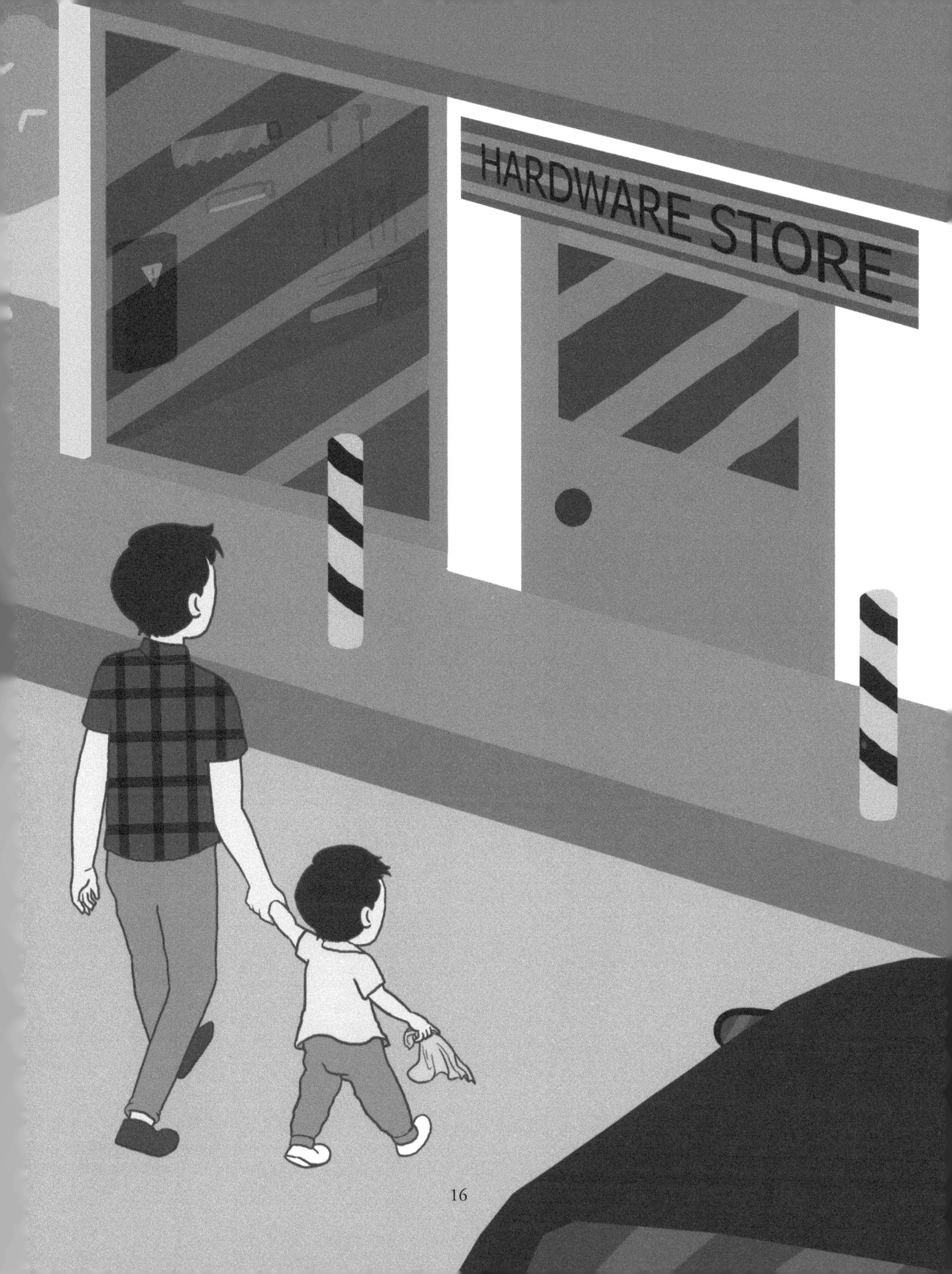
HARDWARE STORE

Daddy's little helper
yes indeed.

I help daddy out with everything he needs.

Daddy's little helper
when things need measured.

I hold one end
and he reads the other.

Daddy's little helper
when boards need a trim.

I help hold the boards
while Daddy cuts them.

Daddy's little helper
when things get put back together.

I hand Daddy the nails
and he uses the hammer.

Daddy's little helper
I have done my best.

I help put up the tools
so there is no mess.

37

Daddy's little helper
from beginning to end.

Our day is done,
Daddy tucks me in.